SHERLOCK GNOMES

GNOME, SWEET GNOME

Adapted by Tina Gallo
Illustrated by Jenny Yoon

Simon Spotlight
New York   London   Toronto   Sydney   New Delhi

SIMON SPOTLIGHT
An imprint of Simon & Schuster Children's Publishing Division
1230 Avenue of the Americas, New York, New York 10020
This Simon Spotlight paperback edition February 2018
TM & © 2018 Paramount Pictures. All Rights Reserved.
All rights reserved, including the right of reproduction in whole or in part in any form.
SIMON SPOTLIGHT and colophon are registered trademarks of Simon & Schuster, Inc.
For information about special discounts for bulk purchases, please contact
Simon & Schuster Special Sales at 1-866-506-1949 or
business@simonandschuster.com.
Manufactured in the United States of America 0318 LAK
10 9 8 7 6 5 4 3
ISBN 978-1-5344-1054-1
ISBN 978-1-5344-1055-8 (eBook)

Hello. My name is Sherlock Gnomes. But then, you probably knew that already, because I am the world's first consulting detective and sworn protector of London's garden gnomes. I'm here to introduce you to some of the gnomes and characters who reside with me in London. I've been chosen to do this because I am the smartest person in the town, if I say so myself. Are you ready? Great. Let's begin.

GNOMEO

We begin with Gnomeo. Gnomeo is a pleasant enough gnome, hopelessly in love with Juliet. He is always saying extremely corny things to her like, "I think it's the most beautiful garden in the world because *you're* standing in it." *Gah*. He once risked getting smashed to death just to get Juliet her favorite flower after they had a fight!

Gnomeo and Juliet wanted to help me solve my latest case—the missing gnomes in London—but Gnomeo got impatient with me when I wouldn't reveal my plan. He told Juliet the two of them should go off on their own and solve it without me. The nerve! Then he became upset with Juliet when she chose to work with me, instead of teaming up with him. But that's ridiculous. Who would ever choose to work with anyone else when *I* was available?

GNOMEO AND JULIET'S FAVORITE FLOWER
THE CUPID'S ARROW ORCHID

JULIET

Ah, the lovely Juliet. Most people are taken by her beauty and don't realize how smart and tough she truly is. She adores Gnomeo (for reasons I simply cannot fathom), and she also has an excellent work ethic. I respect her because she is a strong, independent female. She once said, "A man doesn't make you strong. But the right partner can make you stronger."

When Juliet and I were traveling to Traitors' Gate, we needed to ride the subway. We jumped onto the subway car bumper, but I was hit by a plastic bag, and I nearly fell off. Juliet grabbed me in the nick of time! I respect Juliet a lot, and I suppose I owe her my life. Please don't ever tell her I said that.

LADY BLUEBURY

Lady Bluebury is Gnomeo's mother. She and Lord Redbrick (whom you haven't met yet, but you will soon—patience, please) are the leaders of the garden. However, they have realized it is time for them to retire. They have chosen Gnomeo and Juliet to take over for them and to be in charge. Lady Bluebury loves her son Gnomeo, and he loves her. She's the gnome he turns to whenever he is in trouble.

LORD REDBRICK

Lord Redbrick is Juliet's father. He is always telling her to be careful and that she might fall and hurt herself or get chipped. Silly man. When will he realize that Miss Juliet is the strongest gnome in the garden? He considered putting off his retirement until the new garden was in shape, but Lady Bluebury talked him out of it. He gave Juliet some excellent advice: "I've always put the garden first. To be a good leader you can't get distracted." It doesn't take a detective to figure out where Juliet got her leadership skills!

WATSON

Dr. Watson is my partner. We are the sworn protectors of London's garden gnomes, but lately Watson has become *awfully* sensitive. He keeps saying ridiculous things about my treating him less like a partner and more like an assistant. I don't know where he got *that* idea . . . except maybe it's because I never let him finish a sentence or use any of his ideas. Do you think that might be the reason? Hmmm. I may have to think about this.

NANETTE

Nanette is a garden frog and Juliet's best friend. When Gnomeo and Juliet have an argument, Nanette is the first person Gnomeo goes to for advice on how to smooth things over. Nanette doesn't understand what Juliet sees in Gnomeo, and I agree with her. Nanette is quite strong for a frog. When she and all the other garden gnomes were kidnapped, Gnomeo's pal Benny tried to save her. But Nanette ended up saving *him*! She just tossed him over her shoulder as if he were as light as a feather. She has no patience for romantic nonsense. I like that in a frog!

IRENE ADLER

Irene Adler is in charge of Doyle's Doll Museum. She had a clue that I desperately needed to solve my case, but she refused to give it to me because I treated her horribly. Irene got along very well with Juliet and gave her the clue I needed. Irene also told Juliet that when Juliet saved the day, she was to return and tell Irene all about it. When *Juliet* saved the day? When I, Sherlock Gnomes, the greatest detective mastermind in the world, am around, how could Juliet be the one to save the day? Can you imagine such a thing? Preposterous!

BENNY

Benny is Gnomeo's best friend. He is secretly (or maybe not so secretly) in love with Juliet's best friend, Nanette. I mean, the gnome uses a photo of himself and Nanette as a screen saver! He supports Gnomeo in every way possible. He loves computers and electronics and making up ridiculous code names. Gnomeo gave Benny the code name "Tiny Dancer"! I doubt he has a chance with Nanette, but we shall see. Stranger things have happened.

MORIARTY

Moriarty is my archenemy. Why? Because he is the only ornament in the world who is as brilliant as I am. Eight gardens of gnomes have vanished into thin air without leaving a clue behind—not so much as a single footprint. But when I plotted the locations of the gnome abductions on a map, I saw they made a pattern—the letter *M*! Moriarty left his initial as a message to me. Oh, how I *despise* Moriarty! I must catch him. There isn't room for two geniuses in London. One of us has to go, and it's not going to be me!

THE GARGOYLES

These are the gargoyles. Hideous creatures, are they not? Usually gargoyles are decorative objects on top of buildings. They look scary, but they're all bark and no bite. These garish gargoyles aren't just decorative—they're dangerous. They work for Moriarty, and they are on a mission to destroy me! They might succeed if I do not work things out with Dr. Watson and find a way to stop this madness. As brilliant as I am, I still need help once in a while. (But don't ever tell Watson I said that.)

Well, now our tour has come to an end. I hope you have enjoyed learning about all the gnomes in my town. But of course you did. There's no one who gives more interesting tours than me. Now I must be off to solve another unsolvable case. Good-bye!